Table of content

A day at the beach

A beach is an area of sand or small stones around the sea. I spent a day at Marina Beach in Chennai when I went there with my family on vacations. It was one of the best days of my life. I always wanted to visit the beach because it is a lot of fun.

Before we reached the beach, we bought caps and swimming dresses at the shops. When we reached the beach, I was so excited because everyone was enjoying the sea. Other children were playing with sand.

The beach was surrounded by dense trees and it was very clean. My mother sat on the sand under a tree and took out a book to read. My sister and I went to play with the water in the sea. We splashed water on each other and enjoyed the sea waves when they made us go up and down. After some time, we came back. Then I and my sister made a sandcastle. I also collected shells on the beach and we decorated the castle with them.

We bought fruits on the beach and also drank coconut water after that. When it was evening, we saw the setting sun. It looked like the sun was going inside the sea. We took a lot of pictures of this scene.

The beach became more splendid when the sky turned red. After six o'clock, we went to the changing room and took bath and changed our clothes because the guards did not allow us to be on the beach after sunset. We came back to our hotel and we all talked about our day. We all were so happy because the day was well spent.

Different between beach and ocean

Beach vs. Ocean

Knowing the difference between an ocean and a beach is not that tough. Oceans are so huge that it is acceptable to assume that they are just one continuous body of water that surrounds the entire planet. It occupies more than 70% of the planet's surface due to its size. If you think about it, the Earth contains one large body of water that has been separated into five smaller oceanic bodies, the Atlantic, Indian, Pacific, Southern, and Arctic Oceans, for the purposes of territorial nomenclature. Different seas are further separated into these various oceans.

Oceans are enormous in size and typically reach depths of more than 3,000 meters. Due to the amount of salt in the water, it is also a highly salinized water body. Additionally, due to this enormous quantity of water, the ocean's deep waters are home to a wide variety of marine life.

The biosphere depends heavily on the oceans. In addition to controlling wind and climatic patterns, it also affects the amount of rainfall experienced worldwide.

The ocean is neither white nor blue in color. The ocean is actually a slightly blue body of water, not because it reflects the beautiful blue sky as is commonly believed, but rather because of the red photons that the water molecules absorb from light.

Unlike the ocean, beaches are landforms. They form a part of the shoreline of several bodies of water may it be a lake, a sea or even an ocean. As a landform, beaches have many particles of different rock types like pebbles, gravels, shingles, cobblestones, and of course sand. The action of the sea's waves causes a change in the sediments along the coastal areas. Thus, beaches are either formed or destroyed by these waves. The said particles of rocks are not permanently fixed to an area of land because they are actually in a way 'just' suspended. In addition, beaches have become one of the best hot spots for recreation through the years.

All in all
1.
Oceans are the biggest bodies of water in the planet while beaches are landforms.

2.
There are significantly a lot more marine plants and animals living within the oceans compared to those at the beach.

3.

Oceans are slight blue in color while beaches depend on the color of the type of rock washed towards the shore.

A beach is a landform alongside a body of water which consists of loose particles. The particles composing a beach are typically made from rock, such as sand, gravel, shingle, pebbles, etc., or biological sources, such as mollusc shells or coralline algae. Sediments settle in different densities and structures, depending on the local wave action and weather, creating different textures, colors and gradients or layers of material.

St Oswalds Bay, Dorset, England. Wild sand and shingle beaches are shaped and maintained naturally by wave actions.

Recreational beaches, such as this one on the Gold Coast of Australia, can be shaped and maintained by beach nourishment projects.

A summer tourism at the Yyteri Beach in Pori, Finland.
Though some beaches form on inland freshwater locations such as lakes and rivers, most beaches are in coastal areas where wave or current action deposits and reworks sediments. Erosion and changing of beach geologies happens through natural processes, like wave action and extreme weather events. Where wind conditions are correct, beaches can be backed by coastal dunes which offer protection and regeneration for the beach. However, these natural forces have become more extreme due to climate change, permanently altering beaches at very rapid rates. Some estimates describe as much as 50 percent of the earth's sandy beaches disappearing by 2100 due to climate-change driven sea level rise.

Sandy beaches occupy about one third of global coastlines. These beaches are popular for recreation, playing important economic and cultural roles—often driving local tourism industries. To support these uses, some beaches have man-made infrastructure, such as lifeguard posts, changing rooms, showers, shacks and bars. They may also have hospitality venues (such as resorts, camps, hotels, and restaurants) nearby or housing, both for permanent and seasonal residents.

Human forces have significantly changed beaches globally: direct impacts include bad construction practices on dunes and coastlines, while indirect human impacts include water pollution, plastic pollution and coastal erosion from sea level rise and climate change. Some coastal management practices are designed to preserve or restore natural beach processes, while some beaches are actively restored through practices like beach nourishment.

Marine debris on a beach in Hawaii.

Wild beaches, also known as undeveloped or undiscovered beaches, are not developed for tourism or recreation. Preserved beaches are important biomes with important roles in aquatic or marine biodiversity, such as for breeding grounds for sea turtles or nesting areas for seabirds or penguins. Preserved beaches and their associated dune are important for protection from extreme weather for inland ecosystems and human infrastructure.

Beach evolution

Quartz sand particles and shell fragments from a beach. The primary component of typical beach sand is quartz, or silica ($SiO2$).

Sand and shingle is scoured, graded and moved around by the action of waves and currents

Beach formed on a wild, untamed rocky coastline

Beaches are the result of wave action by which waves or currents move sand or other loose sediments of which the beach is made as these particles are held in suspension. Alternatively, sand may be moved by saltation (a bouncing movement of large particles). Beach materials come from erosion of rocks offshore, as well as from headland erosion and slumping producing deposits of scree. A coral reef offshore is a significant source of sand particles. Some species of fish that feed on algae attached to coral outcrops and rocks can create substantial quantities of sand particles over their lifetime as they nibble during feeding, digesting the organic matter, and discarding the rock and coral particles which pass through their digestive tracts.

The composition of the beach depends upon the nature and quantity of sediments upstream of the beach, and the speed of flow and turbidity of water and wind. Sediments are moved by moving water and wind according to their particle size and state of compaction. Particles tend to settle and compact in still water. Once compacted, they are more resistant to erosion. Established vegetation (especially species with complex network root systems) will resist erosion by slowing the fluid flow at the surface layer. When affected by moving water or wind, particles that are eroded and held in suspension will increase the erosive power of the fluid that holds them by increasing the average density, viscosity, and volume of the moving fluid.

Coastlines facing very energetic wind and wave systems will tend to hold only large rocks as smaller particles will be held in suspension in the turbid water column and carried to calmer areas by longshore currents and tides. Coastlines that are protected from waves and winds will tend to allow finer sediments such as clay and mud to precipitate creating mud flats and mangrove forests. The shape of a beach depends on whether the waves are constructive or destructive, and whether the material is sand or shingle. Waves are constructive if the period between their wave crests is long enough for the breaking water to recede and the sediment to settle before the succeeding wave arrives and breaks.

Fine sediment transported from lower down the beach profile will compact if the receding water percolates or soaks into the beach. Compacted sediment is more resistant to movement by turbulent water from succeeding waves. Conversely, waves are destructive if the period between the wave crests is short. Sediment that remains in suspension when the following wave crest arrives will not be able to settle and compact and will be more susceptible to erosion by longshore currents and receding tides. The nature of sediments found on a beach tends to indicate the energy of the waves and wind in the locality.

Constructive waves move material up the beach while destructive waves move the material down the beach. During seasons when destructive waves are prevalent, the shallows will carry an increased load of sediment and organic matter in suspension. On sandy beaches, the turbulent backwash of destructive waves removes material forming a gently sloping beach. On pebble and shingle beaches the swash is dissipated more quickly because the large particle size allows greater percolation, thereby reducing the power of the backwash, and the beach remains steep. Compacted fine sediments will form a smooth beach surface that resists wind and water erosion.

During hot calm seasons, a crust may form on the surface of ocean beaches as the heat of the sun evaporates the water leaving the salt which crystallises around the sand particles. This crust forms an additional protective layer that resists wind erosion unless disturbed by animals or dissolved by the advancing tide. Cusps and horns form where incoming waves divide, depositing sand as horns and scouring out sand to form cusps. This forms the uneven face on some sand shorelines. White sand beaches look white because the quartz or eroded limestone in the sand reflects or scatters sunlight without absorbing other colors.

Sand colors

Depiction of sands:
glass, dune, quartz
volcanic, biogenic coral, pink coral
volcanic, garnet, olivine
The composition of the sand varies depending on the local minerals and geology. Some of the types of sand found in beaches around the world are:

White sand: Mostly made of quartz and limestone , it can also contain other minerals like feldspar and gypsum .
Light-colored sand: This sand gets its color from quartz and iron ,[5] and is the most common sand color in Southern Europe and other regions of the Mediterranean Basin , such as Tunisia .

Tropical white sand: On tropical islands, the sand is composed of calcium carbonate from the shells and skeletons of marine organisms, like corals and mollusks , as found in Aruba .
Pink coral sand: Like the above, is composed of calcium carbonate and gets its pink hue from fragments of coral, such as in Bermuda and the Bahama Islands .
Black sand: Black sand is composed of volcanic rock, like basalt and obsidian, which give it its gray-black color. Hawaii 's Punaluu Beach, Madeira's Praia Formosa and Fuerteventura's Ajuy beach are examples of this type of sand.
Red sand: This kind of sand is created by the oxidation of iron from volcanic rocks. Santorini 's Kokkini Beach or the beaches on Prince Edward Island in Canada are examples of this kind of sand.
Orange sand: Orange sand is high on iron. It can also me a combination of orange limestone, crushed shells, and volcanic deposits.[6] Ramla Bay in Gozo , Malta or Porto Ferro in Sardinia are examples of each, respectively.
Green sand: In this kind of sand, the mineral olivine has been separated from other volcanic fragments by erosive forces. A famous example is Hawaii's Papakolea Beach , which has sand containing basalt and coral fragments. Olivine beaches have high potential for carbon sequestration , and artificial greensand beaches are being explored for this process by Project Vesta .
Types of beach sand

Fine, white sand made up of pure quartz in Hyams Beach, New South Wales, Australia.

Types of beach

We all adore beaches, don't we? The ultimate beach resort has a chilling quality brought on by walking on white, soft sand, hearing the sound of the waves, and being surrounded by beautiful scenery.

Being near a beach allows you to participate in a variety of water sports and activities, including deep-sea diving, deep-sea boating, surfing, and kayaking. These pursuits keep you fit and active in addition to being enjoyable.

There is even more of a motive for you to visit a beach if you enjoy seafood! You can eat wonderful, fresh fish if you're near the sea. With your loved ones, you can capture large fish and enjoy the "catch of the day" to the fullest!

Folks, that's not all. You can also spend some quality time with your family at the beach. You may plan a wonderful picnic, take priceless pictures with each other, and enjoy delicious refreshments like sandwiches and chips while you're together. Beaches are the best location for nature enthusiasts to take in the scenery. Beautiful sky, palm palms, ocean waves, a calming breeze, breathtaking sunrises and sunsets, and so much more can only be experienced when you visit a beach for real.

Despite the fact that we are all beach lovers, many people are unaware of the different types of beaches. If you travel, you'll learn that there are several types of beaches all around the world. You can learn about them all without leaving your home, so don't worry.

1 Sandy Beaches

Sand is the most traditional component of beaches, making sandy beaches the most recognizable beach type. Sand is responsible for our fond recollections of building sandcastles and sand angels. Since that is what we all so fondly connect with beaches. However, at this point, the question of how sand is made emerges.

To begin with, sand is made of rocks and minerals that have been broken up into minuscule fragments by waves and tides. Sand is produced largely as a result of coastal erosion. Sand formation is influenced by the types of rocks present at a beach as well as the local ocean currents. Sand is often created from feldspar and quartz that are produced by igneous or metamorphic processes.

According to studies, feldspar and quartz are the sources of light brown sand. Dark brown sand is a result of the geographic prevalence of iron oxide. The sand on some beaches with the greatest concentrations of iron oxide can even take on a stunning crimson hue. Canada's Prince Edward Island is one such sand beach.

Below, some common sand beach varieties are covered in more detail.

2. White Sand Beaches

There is no disputing that everyone who enjoys the beach adores beaches with fine, smooth white sand. And there can be a number of general and individual causes for that. However, it is indescribably lovely how they contrast with the glistening waters and heavenly sky. Every day, people from all over the world visit white sand beaches to stroll around, look for seashells, relax alone, or simply have fun with their companions.

Some of the white sand beaches are said to be composed of fish feces, according to legend. Nevertheless, not all white sand beaches include fish sediment. Some of these Florida beaches also include quartz that has been ground up. However, if the sandy beach you visit is surrounded by coral reefs, the sand there was probably created by parrotfish.

Koh Lipe in Thailand, Mayan Beach in Mexico, Pernambuco in Brazil, Whitsundays in Australia, and Bora Bora in French Polynesia are a few of the world's most picturesque white sand beaches.

3. Pink Sand Beaches

If this is the first time you've heard of pink sand beaches, it's quite normal. This is due to how uncommon these beaches are. Everyone's first thought when viewing pink sand beaches is, "What gives the sand its bubblegum color?" According to research, the pink hue of these beaches is caused by the millions of tiny fragments of shattered coral shells and calcium carbonate minerals (left behind by a type of algae – forams).

As previously said, pink sand beaches are rather rare; some well-known pink sand beaches can be found in Greece, Maui, Barbuda, the Caribbean Sea, the Bahamas, Indonesia, and the Philippines.

4.Red sand beaches

If we talk about red sand beaches without including Kaihalulu beach in Maui, Hawaii, it won't be fair. This is due to the fact that this beach is renowned across the world for its red sand, earning it the nickname "red sand beach." Sand that is red in color suggests that there is a lot of iron in the area. Either the earth contains more iron naturally or it has been deposited by volcanic activity, depending on where you look
The light blue Mediterranean waves contrast well with the bright orange sand. Hike up to Calypso Cave for breathtaking scenery. According to popular belief, this is the same cave that Calypso imprisoned Odysseus in for many years as her "love slave" in Homer's "The Odyssey."

Porto Ferro Beach in Italy is another fantastic beach with yellow-orange sand worth mentioning. The orange-colored sand on this beach is a result of volcanic deposits, orange limestone, and fragments of shattered shells. If you look attentively, you could notice magnificent sand dunes in the Mediterranean that are home to joyful beachgoers and surfers.

5. Green Sand beaches

Honestly, a beach with green sand is breathtaking!

The only green sand beaches in the United States are Talofofo Beach in Guam and Papakolea Beach in Hawaii, just to be clear. The mineral olivine is found on these beaches, which is the cause of their greenish sand.

Papakolea Beach's brilliant green sand, which is stunningly combined with black and white sand, is its main draw. You may observe that some sand patches are greener than others if you look closely. Pick a few distinct sand areas and examine the variations between them slowly. You can also go swimming, however occasionally the water may be choppy due to high tides. Keep in mind, too, that there is no covering facility on the beach. Consider bringing your own beach umbrella or hat for sun protection.
   Talofofo Beach in Guam is great for surfing. However, frequent visitors have often remarked that the green sand at this beach is only visible on bright, sunny days. But the picturesque cliffs surrounding the beach make the picnic spot worth the visit.

The best time to visit these green sand beaches is on weekdays or early in the morning of the weekends, especially if you want to escape the crowd.

History of beach

Even in Roman times, wealthy people spent their free time on the coast. They also built large villa complexes with bathing facilities (so-called maritime villas) in particularly beautiful locations. Excavations of Roman architecture can still be found today, for example on the Amalfi Coast near Naples and in Barcola in Trieste.

The development of the beach as a popular leisure resort from the mid-19th century was the first manifestation of what is now the global tourist industry. The first seaside resorts were opened in the 18th century for the aristocracy, who began to frequent the seaside as well as the then fashionable spa towns, for recreation and health. One of the earliest such seaside resorts, was Scarborough in Yorkshire during the 1720s; it had been a fashionable spa town since a stream of acidic water was discovered running from one of the cliffs to the south of the town in the 17th century. The first rolling bathing machines were introduced by 1735.

The opening of the resort in Brighton and its reception of royal patronage from King George IV, extended the seaside as a resort for health and pleasure to the much larger London market, and the beach became a centre for upper-class pleasure and frivolity. This trend was praised and artistically elevated by the new romantic ideal of the picturesque landscape; Jane Austen's unfinished novel Sanditon is an example of that. Later, Queen Victoria's long-standing patronage of the Isle of Wight and Ramsgate in Kent ensured that a seaside residence was considered as a highly fashionable possession for those wealthy enough to afford more than one home.

Seaside resorts for the working class

The extension of this form of leisure to the middle and working classes began with the development of the railways in the 1840s, which offered cheap fares to fast-growing resort towns. In particular, the completion of a branch line to the small seaside town of Blackpool from Poulton led to a sustained economic and demographic boom. A sudden influx of visitors, arriving by rail, led entrepreneurs to build accommodation and create new attractions, leading to more visitors and a rapid cycle of growth throughout the 1850s and 1860s.

The growth was intensified by the practice among the Lancashire cotton mill owners of closing the factories for a week every year to service and repair machinery. These became known as wakes weeks. Each town's mills would close for a different week, allowing Blackpool to manage a steady and reliable stream of visitors over a prolonged period in the summer. A prominent feature of the resort was the promenade and the pleasure piers, where an eclectic variety of performances vied for the people's attention. In 1863, the North Pier in Blackpool was completed, rapidly becoming a centre of attraction for upper class visitors. Central Pier was completed in 1868, with a theatre and a large open-air dance floor.

Many of the popular beach resorts were equipped with bathing machines, because even the all-covering beachwear of the period was considered immodest. By the end of the century the English coastline had over 100 large resort towns, some with populations exceeding 50,000.

Expansion around the world

The development of the seaside resort abroad was stimulated by the well-developed English love of the beach. The French Riviera alongside the Mediterranean had already become a popular destination for the British upper class by the end of the 18th century. In 1864, the first railway to Nice was completed, making the Riviera accessible to visitors from all over Europe. By 1874, residents of foreign enclaves in Nice, most of whom were British, numbered 25,000. The coastline became renowned for attracting the royalty of Europe, including Queen Victoria and King Edward

Continental European attitudes towards gambling and nakedness tended to be more lax than in Britain, so British and French entrepreneurs were quick to exploit the possibilities. In 1863, Charles III, Prince of Monaco, and François Blanc, a French businessman, arranged for steamships and carriages to take visitors from Nice to Monaco, where large luxury hotels, gardens and casinos were built. The place was renamed[citation needed] Monte Carlo.

Commercial sea bathing spread to the United States and parts of the British Empire by the end of the 19th century. The first public beach in the United States was Revere Beach, which opened in 1896. During that same time, Henry Flagler developed the Florida East Coast Railway, which linked the coastal sea resorts developing at St. Augustine, FL and Miami Beach, FL, to winter travelers from the northern United States and Canada on the East Coast Railway. By the early 20th century surfing was developed in Hawaii and Australia; it spread to southern California by the early 1960s. By the 1970s cheap and affordable air travel led to the growth of a truly global tourism market which benefited areas such as the Mediterranean, Australia, South Africa, and the coastal Sun Belt regions of the United States.

Today

Beaches can be popular on warm sunny days. In the Victorian era, many popular beach resorts were equipped with bathing machines because even the all-covering beachwear of the period was considered immodest. This social standard still prevails in many Muslim countries. At the other end of the spectrum are topfree beaches and nude beaches where clothing is optional or not allowed. In most countries social norms are significantly different on a beach in hot weather, compared to adjacent areas where similar behavior might not be tolerated and might even be prosecuted[clarification needed].

In more than thirty countries in Europe, South Africa, New Zealand, Canada, Costa Rica, South America and the Caribbean, the best recreational beaches are awarded Blue Flag status, based on such criteria as water quality and safety provision. Subsequent loss of this status can have a severe effect on tourism revenues.

Beaches are often dumping grounds for waste and litter, necessitating the use of beach cleaners and other cleanup projects. More significantly, many beaches are a discharge zone for untreated sewage in most underdeveloped countries; even in developed countries beach closure is an occasional circumstance due to sanitary sewer overflow. In these cases of marine discharge, waterborne disease from fecal pathogens and contamination of certain marine species are a frequent outcome.

Artificial beaches

Some beaches are artificial; they are either permanent or temporary (For examples, see Copenhagen, Hong Kong, Manila, Monaco, Nottingham, Paris, Rotterdam, Singapore, Tianjin, and Toronto).

The soothing qualities of a beach and the pleasant environment offered to the beachgoer are replicated in artificial beaches, such as "beach style" pools with zero-depth entry and wave pools that recreate the natural waves pounding upon a beach. In a zero-depth entry pool, the bottom surface slopes gradually from above water down to depth. Another approach involves so-called urban beaches, a form of public park becoming common in large cities. Urban beaches attempt to mimic natural beaches with fountains that imitate surf and mask city noises, and in some cases can be used as a play park.

Beach nourishment involves pumping sand onto beaches to improve their health. Beach nourishment is common for major beach cities around the world; however the beaches that have been nourished can still appear quite natural and often many visitors are unaware of the works undertaken to support the health of the beach. Such beaches are often not recognized by consumers as artificial. A famous example of beach nourishment came with the replenishment of Waikīkī Beach in Honolulu, Hawaii, where sand from Manhattan Beach, California was transported via ship and barge throughout most of the 20th century in order to combat Waikiki's erosion problems. The Surfrider Foundation has debated the merits of artificial reefs with members torn between their desire to support natural coastal environments and opportunities to enhance the quality of surfing waves. Similar debates surround beach nourishment and snow cannon in sensitive environments.

Restrictions on access

Further information: Freedom to roam

Public access to beaches is restricted in some parts of the world. For example, most beaches on the Jersey Shore are restricted to people who can purchase beach tags. Many beaches in Indonesia, both private and public, require admission fees. Some beaches also restrict dogs for some periods of the year.

- Private beaches

Private beaches may belong to owners of abutting land, or neighborhood associations. Signs are usually posted the entrance. A permit or special use occasion event may be granted upon executing the proper channels to legally obtain one.

In some places, such as Florida, it is not always clear which parts of a beach are public or private.

- Public beaches

The first public beach in the United States opened on 12 July 1896, in the town of Revere, Massachusetts, with over 45,000 people attending on the opening day. The beach was run bay the Metropolitan Parks Commission and the new beach had a bandstand, public bathhouses, shade pavilions, and lined by a broad boulevard that ran along the beach.

Public access to beaches is protected by law in the U.S. State of Oregon, thanks to a 1967 state law, the Oregon Beach Bill, which guaranteed public access from the Columbia River to the California state line, "so that the public may have the free and uninterrupted use". Public access to beaches in Hawaii (other than those owned by the federal government) is also protected by state law.

Beach design

Beach access is an important consideration where substantial numbers of pedestrians or vehicles require access to the beach. Allowing random access across delicate foredunes is seldom considered good practice as it is likely to lead to destruction of flora and consequent erosion of the foredunes.

A well-designed beach access should:

- provide a durable surface able to withstand the traffic flow;
- aesthetically complement the surrounding structures and natural landforms;
- be located in an area that is convenient for users and consistent with safe traffic flows;
- be scaled to match the traffic flow (i.e. wide and strong enough to safely carry the size and quantity of pedestrians and vehicles intended to use it);
- be maintained appropriately; and
- be signed and lit to discourage beach users from creating their own alternative crossings that may be more destructive to the beachhead.

Concrete ramp or steps

A concrete ramp should follow the natural profile of the beach to prevent it from changing the normal flow of waves, longshore currents, water and wind. A ramp that is below the beach profile will tend to become buried and cease to provide a good surface for vehicular traffic. A ramp or stair that protrudes above the beach profile will tend to disrupt longshore currents creating deposits in front of the ramp, and scouring behind. Concrete ramps are the most expensive vehicular beach accesses to construct requiring use of a quick-drying concrete or a cofferdam to protect them from tidal water during the concrete curing process. Concrete is favored where traffic flows are heavy and access is required by vehicles that are not adapted to soft sand (e.g. road registered passenger vehicles and boat trailers). Concrete stairs are commonly favored on beaches adjacent to population centers where beach users may arrive on the beach in street shoes, or where the foreshore roadway is substantially higher than the beach head and a ramp would be too steep for safe use by pedestrians. A composite stair ramp may incorporate a central or side stair with one or more ramps allowing pedestrians to lead buggies or small boat dollies onto the beach without the aid of a powered vehicle or winch. Concrete ramps and steps should be maintained to prevent a buildup of moss or algae that may make their wet surfaces slippery and dangerous to pedestrians and vehicles.

Corduroy (beach ladder)

A corduroy road or beach ladder (or board and chain) is an array of planks (usually hardwood or treated timber) laid close together and perpendicular to the direction of traffic flow, and secured at each end by a chain or cable to form a pathway or ramp over the sand dune. Corduroys are cheap and easy to construct and quick to deploy or relocate. They are commonly used for pedestrian access paths and light duty vehicular access ways. They naturally conform to the shape of the underlying beach or dune profile, and adjust well to moderate erosion, especially longshore drift. However, they can cease to be an effective access surface if they become buried or undermined by erosion by surface runoff coming from the beach head. If the corduroy is not wide enough for vehicles using it, the sediment on either side may be displaced creating a spoon drain that accelerates surface runoff and can quickly lead to serious erosion. Significant erosion of the sediment beside and under the corduroy can render it completely ineffective and make it dangerous to pedestrian users who may fall between the planks.

Fabric ramp

Fabric ramps are commonly employed by the military for temporary purposes where the underlying sediment is stable and hard enough to support the weight of the traffic. A sheet of porous fabric is laid over the sand to stabilize the surface and prevent vehicles from bogging. Fabric Ramps usually cease to be useful after one tidal cycle as they are easily washed away, or buried in sediment.

Foliage ramp

A foliage ramp is formed by planting resilient species of hardy plants such as grasses over a well-formed sediment ramp. The plants may be supported while they become established by placement of layers of mesh, netting, or coarse organic material such as vines or branches. This type of ramp is ideally suited for intermittent use by vehicles with a low wheel loading such as dune buggies or agricultural vehicles with large tyres. A foliage ramp should require minimal maintenance if initially formed to follow the beach profile, and not overused.

Gravel ramp

A gravel ramp is formed by excavating the underlying loose sediment and filling the excavation with layers of gravel of graduated sizes as defined by John Loudon McAdam. The gravel is compacted to form a solid surface according to the needs of the traffic. Gravel ramps are less expensive to construct than concrete ramps and are able to carry heavy road traffic provided the excavation is deep enough to reach solid subsoil. Gravel ramps are subject to erosion by water. If the edges are retained with boards or walls and the profile matches the surrounding beach profile, a gravel ramp may become more stable as finer sediments are deposited by percolating water.

Longest beaches in the world

Amongst the world's longest beaches are:

Eighty Mile Beach (220 kilometres [140 mi]) in north-west Australia;
Praia do Cassino (212 kilometres [132 mi]) in Brazil;
Padre Island beach (about 182 kilometres [113 mi]) in Gulf of Mexico, Texas.
Ninety Mile Beach, Victoria (151 kilometres [94 mi]) in Victoria, Australia;
Cox's Bazar, Bangladesh (150 kilometres [93 mi] unbroken);
Playa Novillero beach (about 90 kilometres [56 mi]) in Mexico.
90 Mile Beach in New Zealand (88 kilometres [55 mi]);
Fraser Island beach (about 65 kilometres [40 mi]) in Queensland, Australia;
Troia-Sines Beach (63 kilometres [39 mi]) in Portugal;
the Jersey Shore, 204 km/127 miles; and
Long Beach, Washington (which is about 40 kilometres [25 mi]).

Coast

The coast, also known as the coastline or seashore, is defined as the area where land meets the ocean or as a line that forms the boundary between the land and the ocean or a lake. The Earth has around 620,000 kilometres (390,000 mi) of coastline. Coasts are important zones in natural ecosystems, often home to a wide range of biodiversity. On land, they harbor important ecosystems such as freshwater or estuarine wetlands, which are important for bird populations and other terrestrial animals. In wave-protected areas they harbor saltmarshes, mangroves or seagrasses, all of which can provide nursery habitat for finfish, shellfish, and other aquatic species. Rocky shores are usually found along exposed coasts and provide habitat for a wide range of sessile animals (e.g. mussels, starfish, barnacles) and various kinds of seaweeds. Along tropical coasts with clear, nutrient-poor water, coral reefs can often be found between depths of 1–50 m.

According to a United Nations atlas, 44% of all people live within 150 km (93 mi) of the sea. Because of their importance in society and high concentration of population, the coast is important for major parts of the global food and economic system, and they provide many ecosystem services to humankind. For example, important human activities happen in port cities. Coastal fisheries (commercial, recreational, and subsistence) and aquaculture are major economic activities and create jobs, livelihoods, and protein for the majority of coastal human populations. Other coastal spaces like beaches and seaside resorts generate large revenues through tourism. Marine coastal ecosystems can also provide protection against sea level rise and tsunamis. In many countries, mangroves are the primary source of wood for fuel (e.g. charcoal) and building material. Coastal ecosystems like mangroves and seagrasses have a much higher capacity for carbon sequestration than many terrestrial ecosystems, and as such can play a critical role in the near-future to help mitigate climate change effects by uptake of atmospheric anthropogenic carbon dioxide.

However, the economic importance of coasts makes many of these communities vulnerable to climate change which causes increases in extreme weather and sea level rise, and related issues such as coastal erosion, saltwater intrusion and coastal flooding. Other coastal issues, such as marine pollution, marine debris, coastal development, and marine ecosystem destruction, further complicate the human uses of the coast and threaten coastal ecosystems. The interactive effects of climate change, habitat destruction, overfishing and water pollution (especially eutrophication) have led to the demise of coastal ecosystem around the globe. This has resulted in population collapse of fisheries stocks, loss of biodiversity, increased invasion of alien species, and loss of heathy habitats. International attention to these issues has been captured in Sustainable Development Goal 14 "Life Below Water" which sets goals for international policy focused on preserving marine coastal ecosystems and supporting more sustainable economic practices for coastal communities Likewise, the United Nations has declared 2021-2030 the UN Decade on Ecosystem Restoration, but restoration of coastal ecosystems has received insufficient attention.

Because coasts are constantly changing, a coastline's exact perimeter cannot be determined; this measurement challenge is called the coastline paradox. The term coastal zone is used to refer to a region where interactions of sea and land processes occur. Both the terms coast and coastal are often used to describe a geographic location or region located on a coastline (e.g., New Zealand's West Coast, or the East, West, and Gulf Coast of the United States.) Coasts with a narrow continental shelf that are close to the open ocean are called pelagic coast, while other coasts are more sheltered coast in a gulf or bay. A shore, on the other hand, may refer to parts of land adjoining any large body of water, including oceans (sea shore) and lakes (lake shore).

Sizes

The Earth has around 620,000 kilometres (390,000 mi) of coastline. Coastal habitats, which extend to the margins of the continental shelves, make up about 7 percent of the Earth's oceans, but at least 85% of commercially harvested fish depend on coastal environments during at least part of their life cycle. As of October 2010, about 2.86% of exclusive economic zones were part of marine protected areas.

The definition of coasts varies. Marine scientists think of the "wet" (aquatic or intertidal) vegetated habitats as being coastal ecosystems (e.g. seagrass, salt marsh etc.) whilst some terrestrial scientist might only think of coastal ecosystems as purely terrestrial plants that live close to the seashore (see also estuaries and coastal ecosystems).

While there is general agreement in the scientific community regarding the definition of coast, in the political sphere, the delineation of the extents of a coast differ according to jurisdiction.[citation needed] Government authorities in various countries may define coast differently for economic and social policy reasons.

Exact length of coastline
This section is an excerpt from the Coastline paradox.
The coastline paradox is the counterintuitive observation that the coastline of a landmass does not have a well-defined length. This results from the fractal curve-like properties of coastlines; i e , the fact that a coastline typically has a fractal dimension. The first recorded observation of this phenomenon was by Lewis Fry Richardson and it was expanded upon by Benoit Mandelbrot.

The measured length of the coastline depends on the method used to measure it and the degree of cartographic generalization. Since a landmass has features at all scales, from hundreds of kilometers in size to tiny fractions of a millimeter and below, there is no obvious size of the smallest feature that should be taken into consideration when measuring, and hence no single well-defined perimeter to the landmass. Various approximations exist when specific assumptions are made about minimum feature size.

Formation of Coast
Tides often determine the range over which sediment is deposited or eroded. Areas with high tidal ranges allow waves to reach farther up the shore, and areas with lower tidal ranges produce deposition at a smaller elevation interval. The tidal range is influenced by the size and shape of the coastline. Tides do

not typically cause erosion by themselves; however, tidal bores can erode as the waves surge up the river estuaries from the ocean.

Geologists classify coasts on the basis of tidal range into macrotidal coasts with a tidal range greater than 4 meters (13 feet); mesotidal coasts with a tidal range of 2 to 4 meters (7 to 13 feet); and microtidal coasts with a tidal range of less than 2 meters (7 feet). The distinction between macrotidal and mesotidal coasts is more important. Macrotidal coasts lack barrier islands and lagoons, and are characterized by funnel-shaped estuaries containing sand ridges aligned with tidal currents. Wave action is much more important for determining bedforms of sediments deposited along mesotidal and microtidal coasts than in macrotidal coasts.

Waves erode coastline as they break on shore releasing their energy; the larger the wave the more energy it releases and the more sediment it moves. Coastlines with longer shores have more room for the waves to disperse their energy, while coasts with cliffs and short shore faces give little room for the wave energy to be dispersed. In these areas, the wave energy breaking against the cliffs is higher, and air and water are compressed into cracks in the rock, forcing the rock apart, breaking it down. Sediment deposited by waves comes from eroded cliff faces and is moved along the coastline by the waves. This forms an abrasion or cliffed coast.

Sediment deposited by rivers is the dominant influence on the amount of sediment located in the case of coastlines that have estuaries. Today riverine deposition at the coast is often blocked by dams and other human regulatory devices, which remove the sediment from the stream by causing it to be deposited inland. Coral reefs are a provider of sediment for coastlines of tropical islands.

Like the ocean which shapes them, coasts are a dynamic environment with constant change. The Earth's natural processes, particularly sea level rises, waves and various weather phenomena, have resulted in the erosion, accretion and reshaping of coasts as well as flooding and creation of continental shelves and drowned river valleys (rias).

Tides often determine the range over which sediment is deposited or eroded. Areas with high tidal ranges allow waves to reach farther up the shore, and areas with lower tidal ranges produce deposition at a smaller elevation interval. The tidal range is influenced by the size and shape of the coastline. Tides do not typically cause erosion by themselves; however, tidal bores can erode as the waves surge up the river estuaries from the ocean.:421

Geologists classify coasts on the basis of tidal range into macrotidal coasts with a tidal range greater than 4 meters (13 feet); mesotidal coasts with a tidal range of 2 to 4 meters (7 to 13 feet); and microtidal coasts with a tidal range of less than 2 meters (7 feet). The distinction between macrotidal and mesotidal coasts is more important. Macrotidal coasts lack barrier islands and lagoons, and are characterized by funnel-shaped estuaries containing sand ridges aligned with tidal currents. Wave action is much more important for determining bedforms of sediments deposited along mesotidal and microtidal coasts than in macrotidal coasts.

Waves erode coastline as they break on shore releasing their energy; the larger the wave the more energy it releases and the more sediment it moves. Coastlines with longer shores have more room for the waves to disperse their energy, while coasts with cliffs and short shore faces give little room for the wave energy to be dispersed. In these areas, the wave energy breaking against the cliffs is higher, and air and water are compressed into cracks in the rock, forcing the rock apart, breaking it down. Sediment deposited by waves comes from eroded cliff faces and is moved along the coastline by the waves. This forms an abrasion or cliffed coast.

Sediment deposited by rivers is the dominant influence on the amount of sediment located in the case of coastlines that have estuaries. Today riverine deposition at the coast is often blocked by dams and other human regulatory devices, which remove the sediment from the stream by causing it to be deposited inland. Coral reefs are a provider of sediment for coastlines of tropical islands.

Like the ocean which shapes them, coasts are a dynamic environment with constant change. The Earth's natural processes, particularly sea level rises, waves and various weather phenomena, have resulted in the erosion, accretion and reshaping of coasts as well as flooding and creation of continental shelves and drowned river valleys (rias).

Tourism

Coasts, especially those with beaches and warm water, attract tourists often leading to the development of seaside resort communities. In many island nations such as those of the Mediterranean, South Pacific Ocean and Caribbean, tourism is central to the economy. Coasts offer recreational activities such as swimming, fishing, surfing, boating, and sunbathing.

Growth management and coastal management can be a challenge for coastal local authorities who often struggle to provide the infrastructure required by new residents, and poor management practices of construction often leave these communities and infrastructure vulnerable to processes like coastal erosion and sea level rise. In many of these communities, management practices such as beach nourishment or when the coastal infrastructure is no longer financially sustainable, managed retreat to remove communities from the coast

Ecosystem services

Estuarine and marine coastal ecosystems are both marine ecosystems. Together, these ecosystems perform the four categories of ecosystem services in a variety of ways: "Regulating services" include climate regulation as well as waste treatment and disease regulation and buffer zones. The "provisioning services" include forest products, marine products, fresh water, raw materials, biochemical and genetic resources. "Cultural services" of coastal ecosystems include inspirational aspects, recreation and tourism, science and education. "Supporting services" of coastal ecosystems include nutrient cycling, biologically mediated habitats and primary production.

Coasts and their adjacent areas on and offshore are an important part of a local ecosystem. The mixture of freshwater and saltwater (brackish water) in estuaries provides many nutrients for marine life. Salt marshes, mangroves and beaches also support a diversity of plants, animals and insects crucial to the food chain. The high level of biodiversity creates a high level of biological activity, which has attracted human activity for thousands of years. Coasts also create essential material for organisms to live by, including estuaries, wetland, seagrass, coral reefs, and mangroves. Coasts provide habitats for migratory birds, sea turtles, marine mammals, and coral reefs.

Types of ecosystem

Emergent coastline

According to one principle of classification, an emergent coastline is a coastline that has experienced a fall in sea level, because of either a global sea-level change, or local uplift. Emergent coastlines are identifiable by the coastal landforms, which are above the high tide mark, such as raised beaches. In contrast, a submergent coastline is one where the sea level has risen, due to a global sea-level change, local subsidence, or isostatic rebound. Submergent coastlines are identifiable by their submerged, or "drowned" landforms, such as rias (drowned valleys) and fjords

Concordant coastline

According to the second principle of classification, a concordant coastline is a coastline where bands of different rock types run parallel to the shore. These rock types are usually of varying resistance, so the coastline forms distinctive landforms, such as coves. Discordant coastlines feature distinctive landforms because the rocks are eroded by the ocean waves. The less resistant rocks erode faster, creating inlets or bay; the more resistant rocks erode more slowly, remaining as headlands or outcroppings.

Other coastal categories

- A cliffed coast or abrasion coast is one where marine action has produced steep declivities known as cliffs.
- A flat coast is one where the land gradually descends into the sea.
- A graded shoreline is one where wind and water action has produced a flat and straight coastline.

Threats to Beaches

Coastal Erosion

The most significant threat to beaches is natural coastal erosion. Coastal erosion is the natural process of the beach moving due to waves, storms, and wind. Beaches that experience consistent coastal erosion are said to be in retreat.

Coastal erosion can be influenced by weather systems. Beaches on the island nation of Tuvalu, in the South Pacific, were retreating very quickly in the 1990s. Meteorologists linked this to the weather system known as the El Nino-Southern Oscillation (ENSO). As ENSO events slowed, Tuvalu's beaches began to recover.

People respond to coastal erosion in different ways. For years, coastal erosion threatened the Cape Hatteras Lighthouse, on Hatteras Island in the U.S. state of North Carolina. The Cape Hatteras Lighthouse is the tallest lighthouse in the United States. For more than 100 years, it has warned ships of the low-lying sandbars and islands known as the Outer Banks. Coastal erosion made the beach beneath the lighthouse unstable. In 2000, the entire lighthouse was moved 870 meters (2,870 feet) inland.

People also combat coastal erosion with seawalls. These large structures, built of rock, plastic, or concrete, are constructed to prevent sand and other beach material from drifting away. Residents of Sea Gate, a community in Coney Island, New York, for instance, invested in a series of seawalls to protect their homes from powerful storms and waves from the Atlantic Ocean.

However, shifting sand is a natural part of the beach ecosystem. Seawalls may protect one section of beach while leaving another with little sand. Seawalls can also increase the speed at which beaches retreat. When tides and waves hit massive seawalls instead of beaches, they bounce back to the ocean with more energy. This tidal energy causes the sand in front of a seawall to erode much more quickly than it would without the seawall.

Hurricane Sandy was a deadly storm that struck the East Coast of the United States in October 2012. Many of the seawalls of Sea Gate crumbled, and more than 25 homes were lost.

Sea Level Rise

Beaches are also threatened by sea level rise. Sea levels have been gradually rising for many years, drowning some beaches completely.

New Moore Island, for example, was a small, uninhabited island in the Bay of Bengal. Both India and Bangladesh claimed the island, which was little more than a strip of sandy beach. In March 2010, rising sea levels drowned the island completely. New Moore Island is now a sandbar.

Development

Although the natural forces of wind and water can dramatically change beaches over many years, human activity can speed up the process. Dams, which block river sediment from reaching beaches, can cause beaches to retreat. In some places, large quantities of sand have been removed from beaches for use in making concrete.

Development threatens the natural landscape of beaches. People develop homes and businesses near beaches for many reasons. Beaches are traditional tourist destinations. Places like the U.S. state of

Hawaii, the island nation of Tahiti, and the islands of Greece are all economically dependent on tourism. Businesses, such as charter boat facilities, restaurants, and hotels, are built on the beach.

People also enjoy living near beaches. Beachfront property is often very highly valued. "The Hamptons" are exclusive beach communities on the eastern end of Long Island, New York. Homes in the Hamptons are some of the most expensive in the United States.

Development can crowd beaches. As more buildings and other facilities are built, beaches become narrower and narrower. The natural, seasonal movement of beach sediment is disrupted. Communities spend millions of dollars digging, or dredging, sand from one place to another in order to keep the beach the same all year.

Disappearing beaches are bad for coastal facilities. Natural beaches reduce the power of waves, wind, and storm surges. Without these barrier beaches, waves and storm surges crash directly into buildings. In 1992, a storm swept away more than 200 homes in the Hamptons. It cost the government more than $80 million to replace the barrier beach.

On Kauai, one of the islands in Hawaii, more than 70 percent of the beach is eroding, partly because of construction of seawalls and jetties, and from clearing out stream mouths. Geologists say Oahu, another Hawaiian island, has lost 25 percent of its shoreline. Tourism is the state's main industry, so disappearing beaches are a major concern. The destruction of Hawaii's beaches could also mean a loss of habitat for many plants and animals, some of which are already endangered.

Beach Pollution

Many beaches, especially in urban areas, are extremely polluted. Waves wash up debris from the ocean, while drainage pipes or rivers deposit waste from inland areas. Some of this waste includes sewage and other toxic chemicals. After strong storms, some beaches are closed. The amount of bacteria, raw sewage, and other toxic chemicals is hazardous to human health. Sometimes, it takes days or even weeks for the toxic waters to wash out to sea.

Beach pollution also includes garbage, such as plastic bags, cans, and other containers from picnics. Medical waste, such as needles and surgical instruments, has even washed up on beaches.

All beach pollution is harmful to wildlife. Birds may choke on small bits of plastic. Marine mammals such as sea lions may become tangled in ropes, twine, or other material. Floating plastic may prevent algae or sea plants from developing. This prevents animals that live in tide pools, such as sea anemones or sea stars, from finding nutrients.

Protecting Beaches

Reducing pollution is an important way to protect beaches. Visitors should never leave trash on the beach or throw it in the ocean.

Beachgoers should also leave wildlife alone—including birds, plants, and seaweed. Taking shells or live animals from the beach destroys the habitat.

People can also protect beaches from excess erosion. Limiting beachfront development can be an important step in protecting the natural landscape of beaches. Along some beaches, areas of vegetation known as "living shorelines" protect the beach ecosystem from erosion and protect the inland area from floods and storm surges.

In some places, machinery is used to dredge sand from the seabed just offshore and return it to the beach. Miami Beach, in the U.S. state of Florida, was restored by this method.

Value of Beaches

Beaches provide many recreational opportunities for millions of people. Boating, fishing, swimming, walking, beachcombing, bird-watching, playing and sunbathing are among the common activities beachgoers enjoy. Beaches provide protection to residents living near the ocean by acting as a buffer against the high winds and waves of powerful storms or rough seas.

Beaches also play an important role in the economy. Spending time at an ocean beach is one of the fastest-growing nature-based outdoor activities in the United States.

NOAA report (2014) based on the economic impacts of marine debris on Orange County, California, found that:
- Marine debris influences the decisions of residents on whether to go to the beach.

- Avoiding beaches with marine debris costs local residents millions of dollars annually.
- Reducing marine debris by 50 percent at beaches in Orange County could generate $67 million in benefits to residents for a 3-month period.

Relaxing Beach Captions

- I live for blue skies and hot days.
- I go where the sunshine is.
- I'm already in vacation mode.
- Dear Beach, I miss you every day.
- The beach is my happy place.
- Life's a beach.
- Happier than a seagull who just scored a french fry.
- Stay salty.
- Paradise found.
- Sandy toes, sun-kissed nose.
- If you're not barefoot, then you're overdressed.
- If you need me, I'll be at the beach.
- Ocean air, salty hair.
- You, me, and the sea.
- Happy as a clam.
- I'm sorry for what I said when I wasn't at the beach yet.
- I love you to the beach and back.
- Catch you on the next wave.
- Eat, beach, sleep, repeat.
- Let your worries drift away.

General Beach Captions

- Sunny days and heatwaves.
- What happens at the beach stays at the beach.
- How many days until summer?
- I want to chase the sun.
- Every body is a beach body.
- Pool hair, don't care.
- I'm a better person when I'm tan.
- Hot dogs or legs?

- I need six-month vacations twice a year.
- Tropical state of mind.
- Less Mondays, more vacay.
- The tans will fade, but the memories will last forever.
- Good times and tan lines.
- I'm going to change the world, but today, I'll just be a mermaid.
- High tides and good vibes.
- Long time no sea.
- Happiness comes in waves.
- A pineapple a day keeps the worries away.
- Mermaid kisses and starfish wishes.
- Dreams are made of sun and sand.
- If you're not barefoot, then you aren't in the right place.
- BRB, quitting everything to be a mermaid.
- I am happy anywhere I can see the ocean.
- Sandy toes, sun-kissed nose.
- Summertime PSA: SPF's your BFF.

Song Lyric Beach Captions

- "Drinking on a beach with you all over me" — Taylor Swift, 'End Game'
- "That's when I make the wish, to swim away with the fish / Is it supposed to be this hot all summer long?" — Miley Cyrus, 'Malibu'
- "Salt air, and the rust on your door / I never needed anything more." — Taylor Swift, 'August'
- "This beach house ain't always been no paradise." — The Carters, 'LOVEHAPPY'
- "Baby, you summertime fine." — J. Cole, 'In The Morning'
- "Tastes like strawberries on a summer evening." — Harry Styles, 'Watermelon Sugar'
- "I'm on an island, even when you're close." — Dua Lipa, 'We're Good'
- "Daisy Dukes, bikinis on top / Sun-kissed skin, so hot we'll melt your popsicle." — Katy Perry, 'California Gurls'
- "Paco Rabanne, A million / Eau de parfum, on your sweater / I'll carry on, summer is done and so are we." — Kim Petras, 'Hillside Boys'
- "On an island in the sun / We'll be playing and having fun / And it makes me feel so fine / I can't control my brain" — Weezer, 'Island In The Sun'
- "Life is a beach, I'm just playin' in the sand."—Lil Wayne, 'Right Above It'
- "I'm surrounded by water/ And I'm not going back again"— Zac Brown Band, 'Toes'

- "You could travel the world/ But nothing comes close/ To the golden coast"—Katy Perry ft. Snoop Dog 'California Gurls'

Conclusion

Information on beach erosion, beach fill, shoreline structures and beach ecology is limited. Some states do have good beach erosion data and a few now have an adequate shoreline structures inventory. States are doing a better job collecting and reporting beach access and surf zone water quality information. Coastal states are providing an increasing amount of beach health information over the Internet.

The indicator information that is available is often confusing. Results are inconsistent within and between states because the studies they are based on use different standards and criteria. Indicator information is also often not easily interpreted by the general public and elected officials.

Because there are significant gaps and limitations in beach health indicators information, it is difficult to know the extent to which our coastal and ocean resources are at risk and how to prioritize responses to the problem areas we can identify.